I Wish I Were a
Furry
Ferret

by Christina Jordan
Illustrated by Gabhor Utomo

magic
wagon

visit us at www.abdopublishing.com

For my firstborn, Emma. My playful, happy, loving girl. —CJ

Published by Magic Wagon, a division of the ABDO Group, 8000 West 78th Street, Edina, Minnesota 55439. Copyright © 2012 by Abdo Consulting Group, Inc. International copyrights reserved in all countries. All rights reserved. No part of this book may be reproduced in any form without written permission from the publisher.

Looking Glass Library™ is a trademark and logo of Magic Wagon.

Printed in the United States of America, North Mankato, Minnesota.
042011
092011
 This book contains at least 10% recycled materials.

Written by Christina Jordan
Illustrations by Gabhor Utomo
Edited by Stephanie Hedlund and Rochelle Baltzer
Cover and interior layout and design by Abbey Fitzgerald

About the Author: Christina Jordan has been an elementary school teacher for 20 years. She also holds a MA in Psychology, and is a wife and a mother of three children. Combining her passion for her profession, education, and her family inspired her to add "author" to her list of accomplishments. The "I Wish I Were. . ." books are Ms. Jordan's first series of children's books.

About the Illustrator: Gabhor Utomo was born in Indonesia, studied art in San Francisco, and worked as an illustrator since he graduated in 2003. He has illustrated a number of children's books and has won several awards from local and national art organizations. He spends his spare time running around the house with his wife and twin daughters.

Library of Congress Cataloging-in-Publication Data

Jordan, Christina.
    I wish I were a furry ferret / by Christina Jordan ; illustrated by Gabhor Utomo.
        p. cm. -- (I wish I were--)
    Summary: A young girl imagines how different her life would be if she were a ferret.
    ISBN 978-1-61641-656-0
    [1. Stories in rhyme. 2. Ferret--Fiction.] I. Utomo, Gabhor, ill. II. Title.
    PZ8.3.J7646Iam 2011
    [E]--dc22   2010048714

I wish I were a furry ferret, the black-footed kind.
My life would be much different, which I really wouldn't mind.

3

My home would be the sprawling space of the North American prairie.
The grass and tunnels underground would protect me from all things scary.

No one would ever say to me, "It's dark now, time for bed."
I'd be nocturnal, as a ferret, and play all night instead.

Playing is not all I'd do when the day is done.
I'd also hunt for prairie dogs until the rising of the sun.

8

I wouldn't need to take ballet to learn to leap and prance.
I'd arch my back, jump around, and do the ferret dance.

My older brother thinks he's fast. But, he'd lose when chasing me.
My skill to race underground would make me hard to see!

But, if I were a furry ferret there would be some things I'd miss,
like swimming at my auntie's pool, where I pretend that I'm a fish.

I'd have a built-in costume—a black bandit furry mask.
But to be in costume every day would bore me pretty fast.

16

One of my favorite things to do is play basketball.
I couldn't do that as a ferret at 18 inches tall.

19

My home would be a burrow way deep down in the ground.
There'd be no room for all my toys or space to play around.

21

Oh, furry ferret, it would be great to run nightly and be free.
But for now, I'm having fun. I'm happy being me!

Fun Ferret Facts

• Ferrets are very playful animals. They like to wrestle with each other. They even have their own "ferret dance."

• Ferrets weigh 1.5 to 2.5 pounds (.7 to 1.1 kg). They are 18 to 25 inches (46 to 64 cm) long.

• Black footed ferrets are obligate carnivores. This means they eat mostly one type of meat. Their main prey is the prairie dog.

• Black-footed ferrets are one of the most endangered species in the world. They are protected by laws and are slowly growing in number.

Glossary

arch - to curve.

burrow - a hole or tunnel dug in the ground by a small animal for shelter.

endangered species - a plant or animal that is in danger of no longer existing because of loss of habitat or other reasons.

nocturnal - an animal that sleeps during the day and is awake at night.

prairie - flat and grassy land.

prance - to dance about.

protect - to keep from harm.

sprawling - wide open and spread out.

Web Sites

To learn more about ferrets, visit ABDO Group online at **www.abdopublishing.com**. Web sites about ferrets are featured on our Book Links page. These links are routinely monitored and updated to provide the most current information available.